Illustrated by Jerrod Maruyama
© 2020 Disney Enterprises, Inc. All rights reserved.

Customer Service: 1-877-277-9441 or customerservice@pikidsmedia.com

Published by Phoenix International Publications, Inc.
8501 West Higgins Road   59 Gloucester Place
Chicago, Illinois 60631   London W1U 8JJ

PI Kids and *we make books come alive* are trademarks of
Phoenix International Publications, Inc., and are registered in the United States.

www.pikidsmedia.com

ISBN: 978-1-5037-5488-1

Louie Likes Basketball

A STORY ABOUT SHARING

we make books come alive®

pi kids **Phoenix International Publications, Inc.**

Chicago • London • New York • Hamburg • Mexico City • Sydney

Huey, Dewey, and Louie are busy looking for Louie's missing basketball.

"Over there!" says Dewey.

"I think I see it—inside that red wagon!"

"**Great!**
I want to practice **dribbling**," says Huey.

"I want to *shoot* baskets," says Dewey.

"Wait a minute," says Louie. "Uncle Donald bought this for my birthday. That makes it **my basketball**! I'm the only one who gets to use it."

"**I have an idea,**" says Huey. "We'll have a shooting contest. Whoever wins gets to play with the basketball."

"**Good idea!**" says Dewey.

"Let's go!"

"OK," says Louie. "But I know that basketball is mine."

"I'll be the ref," says Donald.

Tweeeet!

Huey shoots first.
He makes **one** basket,
then **two** baskets,
then **three** baskets!

Dewey shoots next.
He makes **one** basket,
then **two** baskets,
then **three** baskets!

"So far, it's even,"
says Donald.
It's Louie's turn.
He makes **one** basket,
then **two** baskets...

SWOOSH!

...but before making his third shot, Louie says, "I have a better idea. I'll just keep the basketball! Thanks, guys!"
Then he

BOUNCE

BOUNCE

BOUNCES

the basketball down the driveway.

Huey shouts, **"Hey! Come back here!"**

Dewey stomps his foot and says, **"Give us that ball!"**

Donald says, "Not so fast! If you three can figure out a way to earn some money, then you can buy **two more basketballs**!"

"**OK!**" the boys shout. "**You're on!**"

But first they have to come up with a plan. Should they **mow lawns**? **Wash cars**? **Walk dogs**? Finally, they decide to open a **lemonade stand**!

Mickey and Goofy stop by for lunch.

"I brought us a sandwich **we can share**," says Goofy.

"How can we share **one** sandwich?" asks Louie.

"It's easy," says Goofy, "when the sandwich is

four feet loooong!"

The boys tell Mickey and Goofy about their plan to open a lemonade stand. Now Mickey has an idea. "We're making cookies this afternoon.

We can share them with you to sell at your lemonade stand."

"**Wow, thanks!**" says Louie.
"You betcha!" says Goofy.

"YUM!"

When the cookies are ready, Donald and Goofy do the dishes.

OOops!

Mickey mops the floor.
"When we **share the work**, cleanup is easy!"
says Mickey.

"You know," says Huey, "this **sharing** thing kind of makes sense. That sandwich was yummy."

"And now we have cookies to sell with our lemonade!" Dewey says.

The boys agree to **share the work** for the lemonade stand. Huey makes the sign, Dewey makes the lemonade, and Louie calls for customers.

"Lemonade and cookies for sale!

Step right up!"

At the end of the day, the brothers count the money they made.

"Good job, fellas!"

says Donald. "You made enough
to buy **lots** of basketballs."

"Hey...instead of buying more basketballs, what if we **share** this one? Then we can buy other stuff we want!" says Louie.

"I'd like to get a football!"

"Great idea!" says Dewey.

"I'll get a baseball and a mitt!"

"I'll get a soccer ball!"
says Huey.

"And we can **share**
them all!" says Louie.

At the store, the boys pick out their purchases. They even buy some **tennis balls** for their Uncle Donald!

"Sharing works pretty well, don't you think?" asks Donald.

"You can say that again, Uncle Donald!"

the nephews shout.

"Sharing is the name of the game!"